A Pandemic Adventure

Written by
Robina Brah

Authors Note

A Pandemic Adventure

March 11, 2020, marked the arrival of a global pandemic of the COVID-19 Virus. As a result, the world as we knew it would never be the same. People's mental health, how business is conducted, and how we interact as humans, amongst other things, took their toll. The longer the lockdowns, confusion, and restrictions lasted, the more individuals and communities began to lose hope for a better future.

The repercussions of this pandemic are still with us today and will be for years to come. So, it is hard to say whether this is all over.

I decided to write this book to showcase what businesses may have gone through, as well as how children may have felt during this time. I hope this book can reinforce that although people have different worries beyond today that are hard to go through, we are all in this together even though we are apart.

I hope that the variety of situations discussed within this book will provide children with a well-rounded understanding of others and encourage them to always be kind.

Thank you to everyone who contributed to the process of writing, editing, and creating this book. I look forward to writing many more.

Acknowledgements

A Pandemic Adventure

Written By: Robina Brah
Illustrated By: Madeleine Poole
Edited By: Stephanie Saroff

Thank you to my family and friends for their continuous support throughout this process.

A special thank you to:

- Edward Henry for pushing me to make this the book that it has become, never letting me settle for less, and reminding me that even though I may struggle, that doesn't mean I should quit.
- My parents, Paul and Manjit Brah, for never letting me give up, and for finding my illustrator.
- Madeleine Poole for their creativity, patience, and time spent in creating the illustrations. It was truly a pleasure to work with you, and I look forward to working with you on many more books.
- Stephanie Saroff for the time spent on editing this book in its initial stages, as well as her patience and dedication. I look forward to working together again.
- Vivian Gomide for their time spent on continuous read-throughs of this book and their helpful suggestions.
- Friesen Press Publishing Company for making the publishing process smooth.

Our story begins in a place faraway.
In a village where porcupines live, rest and play.

A porcupine named Peter and his mom called
this their home. They both loved how
they never felt alone.

Peter always wished that weekends would never end. He spent most of his time hanging out with his friends. From morning to night, he would always be gone. He always enjoyed the adventures he was on.

Peter's mom watched the clock until late. She hoped he wouldn't stay out past eight. Peter noticed how late it was starting to get. He remembered that his homework wasn't done yet.

The next day, Peter came home excited from school.
He always found learning new things very cool.

Peter saw his mom and knew something was wrong. He knew her days as a nurse were sometimes long. She was shocked and told Peter about what she had just seen. There was talk about a virus called COVID-19.

With each passing day, more about this was said, such as how far around the world it had quickly spread.

6
FEET
APART

There were rules that said we must stay six feet apart. Wearing masks and washing hands more was just the start. Seeing friends and grandparents was also declined. On top of all that, all schools went online.

For a while it was hard to find learning cool. Peter only saw his friends during online school. Not seeing his friends made him feel sad. Peter's mom wished she knew how to make him feel glad.

It was hard to believe that everything had changed. Not seeing his grandparents on birthdays was strange. Peter's mom wondered how long this would last. Peter's birthday and Christmas had already passed.

Peter was tired of not being someplace new. Going on an adventure is what he thought he should do. Excited to go, he took his mask, bag, and coat. Before he left the house, he left his mom a note.

The wind and rain almost knocked him off his feet. But Peter was not about to accept defeat. He walked through heavy rain and wind for quite a while. Seeing a town ahead is what made him smile.

He made his way into town and there he met Buzzbee. Buzzbee was a bumble-bee who sold great honey. Buzzbee was excited to meet someone new. Little did he know what Peter was going through. Buzzbee knew he had to ask from six feet away. Buzzbee buzzed,

"Hi, what brings you to Whitby today."

Peter took a big deep breath before he could speak

With teary eyes he said, "It's adventure I seek. I needed to escape from what was going on. This virus has been here for way too long."

Buzzbee buzzed with excitement. "Oh my, you are brave!
Just leaving my hive makes me feel so afraid."

Peter sighed, then he said, "What else could I do? I was just so tired of not being someplace new."

Buzzbee went ahead and said, "I know what you mean. Everyday I come to work, and it is hard to believe. Lately things have been hard, and I feel so alone. I run a shop called The Bees Knees all on my own. More and more of my worker bees just want to leave. From nine to five they wear masks, wash their hands, and clean. I have three little bees at home who wish I was there. Right now, I feel that life just really isn't fair. Staying six feet apart has been so hard to do. With everything going on, I just have no clue."

Peter was shocked about what he just found out. He was surprised that Buzzbee didn't start to burn out. Neither of them looked like they knew what to say. They both just agreed that it had been a long day.

Mr. Rich, the largest shop owner in town, walked down the street.
To his surprise, Buzzbee and Peter were there for him to greet.

"Hello, I'm Mr. Rich, It's nice to meet you." Peter and Buzzbee introduced themselves too. Mr. Rich asked if everything was okay. He noticed that they both looked troubled today. They both took a deep breath and said what was wrong. "Lately, it's been hard with everything going on."

Mr. Rich agreed, and said, "I know what you mean. Because of the virus I've had to change my whole routine. I've had to learn how to do everything online. Sometimes I don't leave my shop until after nine. Because my shop is big, things have been very hard. I wish I had more time to spend in my backyard. Everyday I go to work and feel so crummy. I worry about always needing more money. It's been hard to keep my shop open for this long. All I want is for all my stress to be gone. I worry every morning and afternoon. I may have to close down my shop for good soon."

Everyone stopped talking for what felt like a while.
Mr. Rich then asked if they could walk a few miles.

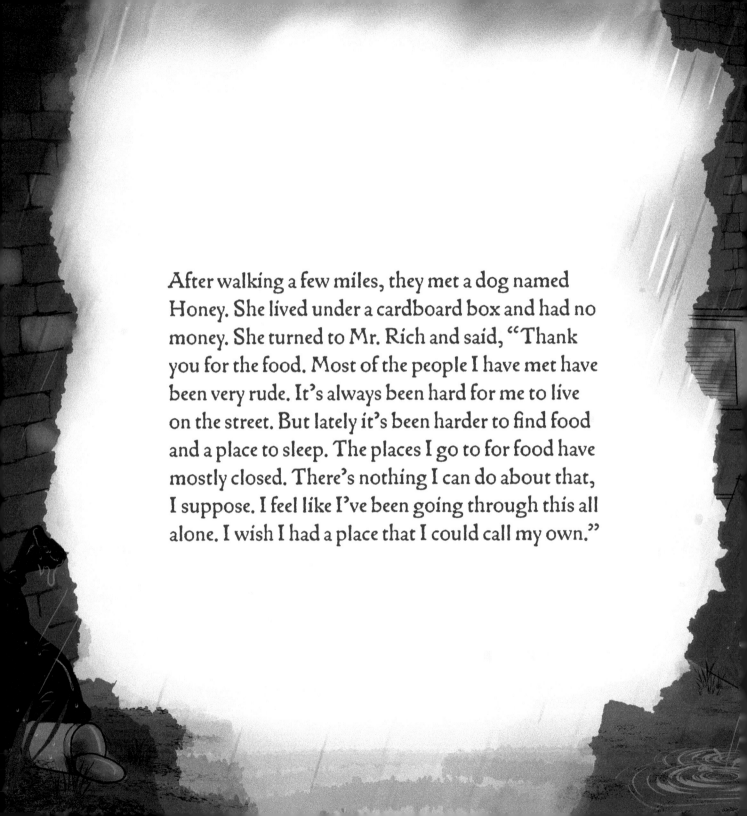

After walking a few miles, they met a dog named Honey. She lived under a cardboard box and had no money. She turned to Mr. Rich and said, "Thank you for the food. Most of the people I have met have been very rude. It's always been hard for me to live on the street. But lately it's been harder to find food and a place to sleep. The places I go to for food have mostly closed. There's nothing I can do about that, I suppose. I feel like I've been going through this all alone. I wish I had a place that I could call my own."

Mr. Rich knew everyone was feeling down. He wished he knew what to say to turn things around. Placing his hand on his chest, he found what to say. He said, "Everyone has worries beyond today. These worries are all different and hard to go through. Even though we are apart, we are together, too."

Now their adventure had come to an end. Peter was sad to say goodbye to his new friends. With a big wave goodbye, they all went different ways. Leaving with the hope of meeting again someday.

Peter found the right road and headed for home. He knew his mom was waiting for him all alone. Peter wondered if his mom has seen his note. The one he had left her before he grabbed his coat. As fast as he could, he made it over the bridge. With each step he took, he was closer to the village.

Meanwhile, Peter's mom came home from working as a nurse. She had one of those days where nothing could have gone worse. At the hospital where she worked it was too busy. At times she would miss lunch and feel very dizzy. With each passing day, more and more people got sick. The rules were always changing really, really quick. She hated wearing so much gear all day. She hoped that one day soon, this would all go away

She was tired and started to yawn. Then she saw Peter's note and was surprised he was gone. She hoped that when he left, he had taken his phone. She was a bit worried and called him to come back home.

As Peter was getting closer, he heard his phone. It was mom telling him to please come back home. Peter said that he could see the village ahead. He also said that he would be home right before bed.

As soon as he got in, he hugged his mom very tight. He said, "I'm sorry, I know leaving home wasn't right."

Peter was excited to have stories to tell. He was so excited he practically yelled. He talked about his new friends and where he had gone. He told her everything he had learned and talked on and on.

Peter had one last thing to say, "Everyone has different worries beyond today. These worries are all different and hard to go through. Although we are apart, we are together, too."

THE END

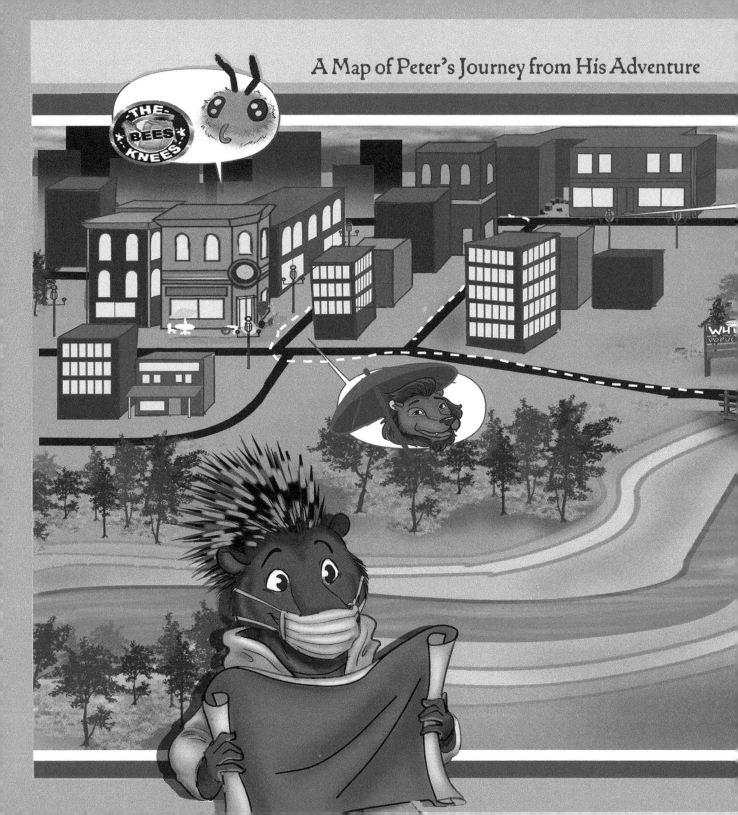

About the Author

Robina Brah has always had a passion for helping, teaching, and inspiring others, -from her community involvement to her leadership roles in business. Her hobbies include running, ultimate frisbee, volunteering, reading, and hiking. Robina has obtained her Bachelor of Arts in Forensic Psychology with a Minor in Criminology and Justice from Ontario Tech University. She was also the Keynote speaker and Ontario Tech University Alumni Association Philanthropic Award Winner for the class of 2017. Robina believes that children can improve their own worlds, and that children's books provide valuable lessons. Robina plans to continue writing books that focus on meaningful life lessons, and positively influence all who read them.

About the Editor

Stephanie Saroff has always had a passion for editing and writing. It has been a dream for her to be a part of helping create content for young readers. The pandemic has challenged us with many changes. Learning from these changes is what will continue to push us forward. There will be more adventures ahead. Stephanie hopes to continue her work in children's books and inspire others along the way. She looks forward to her next adventure.

About the Illustrator

Madeleine Poole is a Canadian illustrator from Ontario, and a graduate from the Animation and Digital Design Program at Durham College. After graduating, they taught a course in 2D Animation, before moving on to work in the film industry as a stereo artist. When they aren't working on personal projects, they can often be found pursuing their own passions, such as playing tabletop games, like Dungeons&Dragons, swimming at the gym, spending time with friends and family, or playfully bothering their cat.

One Printers Way
Altona, MB R0G 0B0
Canada

www.friesenpress.com

Copyright © 2023 by Robina Brah
First Edition — 2023

Illustrated by Madeleine Poole

Edited by Stephanie Saroff

The characters and their situations in this book are a work of fiction and purely the authors imagination. However, elements such as the town the book takes place in (Whitby) and the overall event described (the pandemic) is not fictional.

ISBN
978-1-03-915731-6 (Hardcover)
978-1-03-915730-9 (Paperback)
978-1-03-915732-3 (eBook)

1. JUVENILE FICTION, SOCIAL ISSUES, NEW EXPERIENCE

Distributed to the trade by The Ingram Book Company

CPSIA information can be obtained
at www.ICGtesting.com
Printed in the USA
BVHW010100090323
659876BV00002B/20

9 781039 157309